Love Monster Lulu

She runs out the kitchen
And straight through the door
But does pause to eat
That grape off the floor.

She chases the dog
And chases the cat
But they are having
Nothing of that!

She looks for her sister,
Her father, her mother,
Her aunt, her uncle,
And even her **brother.**

She wants some more love,
A great big bear hug,
A slobbery wet kiss,
A snuggle-y snug.

Where did they go?
Did everyone hide?
She can't seem to find them…
Are they outside?

The love monster's sad–
What can she do?
She's feeling quite bad…

a bit out of her love groove.

The love monster **wails**
And drops to the floor,
Out of sorts
Like never before.

But then to her left,
Without seeing it coming,
The love monster's surprised
By a small special something.

A blue butterfly
That lands on her nose
Then flits down her legs,
Dancing on toes.

Then up to the sky
The butterfly flies–
"But wait! But wait!"
The love monster cries!

"Don't go away,
Don't leave me too...
I have no one to love,
Now not even you!"

Her crying is heard
By her mother and sister,
Barley the dog,
And the family cat Mister.

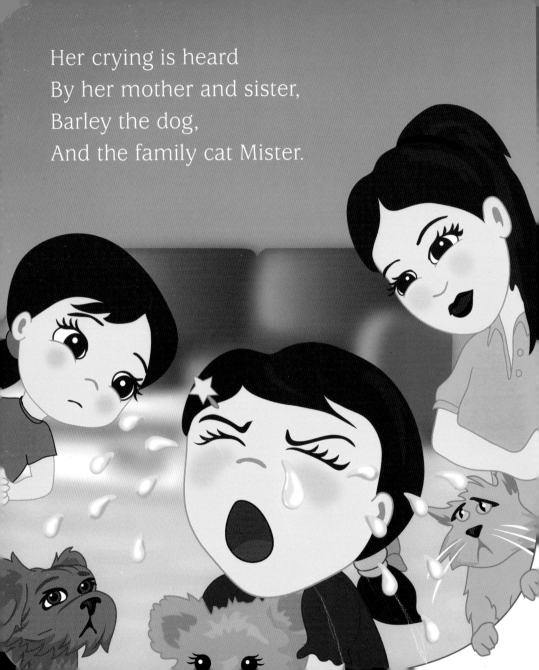

They make a hug sandwich
Till she's filled up with love,
And with a great big smile,
She looks up above.

"Bye Bye Butterfly,
I love you too.
But now that I have my family...

We are social!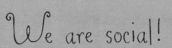

www.facebook.com/mypumpkinheads
www.twitter.com/mypumpkinheads
www.pinterest.com/pumpkinheads

For animated stories and videos, subscribe!
www.youtube.com/mypumpkinheads

For more Pumpkinheads news, books,
games and products, please visit us at:

www.pumpkinheads.com